Timothy Tiger's Terrible Toothache

By Jan Wahl
Illustrated by Lisa McCue Karsten

For Larry and Virginia

A GOLDEN BOOK · NEW YORK
Western Publishing Company, Inc., Racine, Wisconsin 53404

Owtch!

In the middle of the night Timothy Tiger woke up. His tooth hurt.

He got out of bed and walked down the hall to his parents' door. He knocked.

"What is it?" whispered his mother.

"I have a toothache."

"Here is a hot-water bottle," she said. Softly singing, Mother Tiger sang Tim to sleep.

But in the morning it still didn't feel good. Timothy tried to rub it away with his paw.

After breakfast, his sister Eliza tried hard to spin a
magic spell.

This only made him dizzy. He stepped in circles,
right, then left, on the striped rug. The toothache
followed him.

Before Father Tiger went to work, he looked in Tim's mouth. "Open wide...I think it's a job for the dentist, Son."

"I would rather have the toothache," said Tim.

And he went out to play. The sun was shining. Timothy swung on a swing with Eliza. "I don't mind the up! But I do mind the down," he moaned.

Pretty soon he stood at the back door. "It's going to rain. My tooth tells me."

Timothy's mother poured cold mint tea over cotton. "We will put this against your tooth."

The tooth still hurt.

His grandmother drove up.

"Here is what we did for toothache when your father was small."

She dipped a clean bandanna in something called camphor. Now she tied it on his jaw.

The tooth still hurt.

"Maybe it wants to go for a ride in my car," suggested Grandmother.

"Maybe," he groaned.

So Timothy sat on the red seat beside her.

Grandmother drove carefully. Carefully as they went, the car banged over bumps.

"YowEEE!" shouted Timothy loudly.

The car stopped.
"Look where we are!" Grandmother said, whistling.
"This is the dentist's. How nice…"
Nice or not, the two walked in.

The dentist had long flowing whiskers and pearly teeth.

Timothy sat in the chair, and Grandmother sat on a high stool.

Miss Tiger tied a large napkin on him.
The dentist squirted peppermint water in his mouth.
"Mmm, that tastes fine," said Tim.

"Show me where your toothache is," said the dentist. With a shiny little mirror he looked at every tooth. "We need to take a picture."

The dentist put an X-ray film beside the sore tooth.
"Hold still," said Miss Tiger.
Whir, whir, click.

"Ah. Here's the problem…I can fix this," the dentist said.

Something was put over Timothy's nose.

"Take a deep breath," said Miss Tiger.

"Open wide," said somebody.

A machine whizzed.

Funny, soon Timothy was dreaming.
*He rode a merry-go-round horse, and so did
Grandmother—the dentist—and Miss Tiger.
"Take the brass ring!" yelled Grandmother.
He raced the others round and round. Timothy
grabbed the ring. He was the winner!*

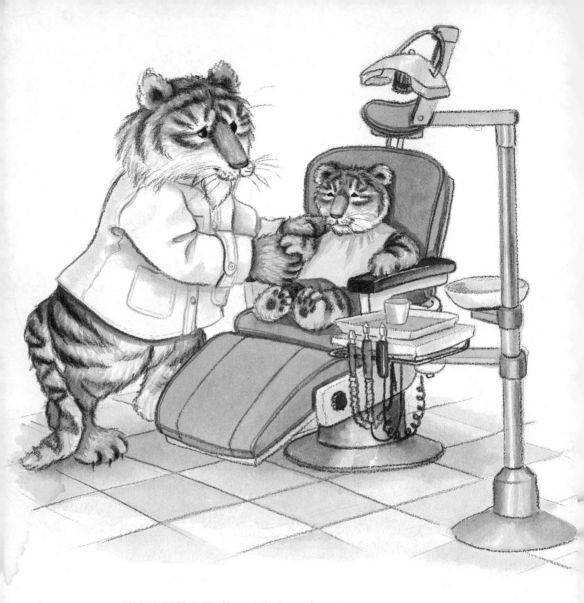

"WAKE UP!" said the dentist.
Slowly Timothy opened his eyes.
    The dentist shook his paw. "Timothy, you took
laughing gas. While you were dreaming we were
working."

Tim asked, "I wasn't on a merry-go-round?"
The dentist showed him his tooth.
Grandmother gave Timothy Tiger a big hairy hug.

On the way home the car bounced on bumps.
Timothy didn't mind.

Rain splashed on the road, and then the sun was
shining again.